HOW TO STEAL A HEART IN 500 KISSES

How to Love #1

ANYTA SUNDAY

Third edition published in 2020 by Anyta Sunday
Buerogemeinschaft ATP24, Am Treptower Park 24, 12435 Berlin

An Anyta Sunday publication
www.anytasunday.com

ISBN 978-3-947909-25-4

Cover Design by Natasha Snow
www.natashasnow.com

Content Edit & Proofread by Lynda Lamb @ Refinery
www.refineryedits.com

Line Edit by HJS Editing
www.hjseditingservices.com

This book contains explicit sexual content.

For Marie,
Thank you for the wonderful prompt.

Chapter One

DYLAN

RAIN SOAKED his jeans and hiking boots. Every running step was a squelch and a splash and a slip through deep puddles and loose stones.

Dylan Halsworth darted down the slippery gravel path toward his counselors and their thirty young campers huddled in cabins at Camp Halsworth.

Lightning sliced through the dark sky. Dylan spun toward the thunderous crack, heart slamming as an ancient oak snapped toward the dining hall—

No, no, no. Right through the kitchen . . .

He'd check the kids first, then cordon off the damage. When would this torrential rain stop? Half the parents had already called, wanting reassurance. He'd convinced most of them not to pick their kids up early.

But now . . .

He gritted his teeth at the oak skeleton protruding from the roof.

A counselor jogged toward him, cursing the downpour. He zipped his mouth on the next f-word—banned at the campsite—and inclined his head. "Is that a *tree* in the dining hall?"

Fucking fuck suited the situation perfectly. Dylan rolled his shoulders and nodded. "The kids?"

"Kids in cabins four to seven are all fine. A bit spooked, but laughing it off."

"One to three and eight to ten?"

"Ronald said his are okay, but there's a small leak in cabin two. He ordered the boys to pack, and I told mine in cabin five to expect company. It'll be good for tonight. Heather said her girls are fine."

Water drizzled down his neck, sluicing a path between his shoulder blades. This damn jacket did no good. He may as well have run out in his pajamas.

"Good." Dylan slapped his counselor on the shoulder. "Back inside with you. I'll figure out a plan for the morning. Keep the kids away from the dining hall."

Jeff nodded and jogged off.

Dylan stomped his boots, splattering muddy water up his pantlegs. He cocked his head to the turbulent sky and yelled his lungs raw.

He sprinted to the dining hall to inspect the damage. Well, shit. What would he do without a kitchen for the rest of the summer?

Thirty kids. Six counselors. And, well—fucking fuck, right?

He couldn't have the kids picked up halfway through summer camp. He'd have to give partial refunds, and . . . well, summer was his prime money-making season.

Dylan slammed a palm against the doorframe.

He moped to his house and shoved his wet clothes in the washing machine. Fresh T-shirt and boxers later, he moved to his study, where a stack of bills glared at him. Electricity. Water. Mortgage payments. Dad's medical bills . . .

He swiveled away from the mounds of paperwork to the view of his camp. Rain pelted the path where he'd learned to ride a bike, tinkered over the shed where he'd first run away, pummeled the trees he used to climb while his dad worked on cars under them.

Generous buyout offers had poured in over the years for this land, but . . .

Dylan gaped at the collapsed kitchen roof, where he used to sit and gaze at the stars reflected in the lake.

He shook his head. Selling his home was not an option. He needed to make sure the camp ran without another hitch.

Camp Halsworth had served campers for generations, and he did not intend to stop now.

He moved to the window. The path lights showed up the sludgy soil—bleak, much like his eyes, hair, and situation.

He'd move contractors in immediately, but a mess like this could take months to fix.

If only there were a kitchen and an indoor hall for wet-weather activities.

Something close by.

Something big enough.

Dylan gazed out across the lake through the drizzling rain.

He groaned, but made the call . . .

Chapter Two

CHRIS

CHRIS TWISTED ONTO his side, sheets tangling around his legs, and stared out his large terrace windows. Thunderous rain shelled against the glass, and someone breathed heavily against his shoulder blade.

An arm draped around Chris's middle, and a nose nuzzled into his neck.

Chris twisted to face Alexander—his hookup.

Alexander smiled and kissed his chest. High-cheekbones, slender form. A good few inches shorter than his own six-one. Blond hair and blue eyes to his brown and brown. Clever as hell, with a cute grin. Chris's late mother would have given him a thumbs-up.

Chris wanted a thumbs-up—he did.

He wanted many things.

Selfish of him, since he already *had* many things. Things money could buy, anyway. A mansion. Three catamarans.

Almost his own lake. He never had to work if he didn't care to. Most of the time, he didn't—unless it was restoring old boats.

Yet he still . . . wanted.

What would it be like to wake up every day to the same person?

Rain thickened, hitting the glass harder. Chris shifted, giving himself some space. "Um, you can stay the night. Avoid the storm."

Alexander raised a brow. "You're different than I expected."

That caught his attention. He fished for a smile and faced the man. "What did you expect?"

Alexander's shoulder rolled with a shrug. "There are rumors about you around town."

Town. Inglewood. Population 500, swelling to 750 over the summer. "Rumors?"

"You never let a date sleep over, and you only do nice things if it's good for you."

Is that how he came across? He rubbed a hand over his jaw like it might erase the sting in his throat.

"Also . . . no, forget it."

"What?"

"You know that stretch of land by the river with that haunted cabin of yours?"

Bennington Way. Chris sat, blanket pooling at his waist. "What about it?"

"Mary says the lease is up for renewal in July, and she'll be leasing it to the local hiking club."

Chris jumped out of bed, snapping his T-shirt off the floor and jerking it on. "She said what?"

Alexander cocked a brow. "Everyone knows you never use it. The cabin's old and rundown."

"Not everyone knows what they're talking about. I'll renew the lease." No matter what it cost him. That plot had been on a long-term lease to his family for fifty years. His grandfather had built that cabin—

He pushed down the memories. The hiking club would tear his cabin down and put up new ones, ones that didn't have history like his did.

"She seemed keen on letting more people use the land."

The phone rang, and Chris lurched for it.

"Who's calling you at midnight?" Alexander asked.

The screen flashed: Dylan Halsworth.

Chris's stomach twisted, and Alexander peeked at the screen, frowning.

Chris slumped against the bed, phone blaring. "The guy across the lake."

"Oh, a neighbor."

"Neighbor is a nice word for what we are."

Alexander cracked a grin. "The guy you flipped off as we docked earlier?"

Chris stared at the still-ringing phone. "The very one. It's how we say hello. Been that way since we were sixteen. He runs summer camps. Still can't steer a damn boat."

"Why do you have his number?"

"To avoid his calls." But Dylan only called when they had business to take care of regarding the lake that separated their properties. The last time Dylan had called, he'd asked him to replace the buoys at the bottleneck. Hadn't been polite about it.

'Course, Chris hadn't been polite about the floodlight Dylan had installed either. Glared right into his bedroom window, that beast. Could've lit a stadium.

Rain pelted the large, hourglass-shaped lake. As a kid, he'd loved that he and Dylan were separated by the narrowest stretch of water, but now . . .

"This Dylan guy might need some neighborly assistance," Alexander said, shuffling closer. "Storm's wild."

"Play the Good Samaritan?" To his nemesis?

The phone stopped ringing, only to start again. Halsworth wouldn't give up.

"I mean," Alexander said, "if there were rumors about how unlikeable *I* was . . ."

Chris blinked hard. *Unlikeable*? That's how the town saw him?

His stomach squeezed. Clumsily, he answered Dylan's call.

Chapter Three

DYLAN

"Sure. You and the kids can use my place. It's plenty big enough."

Dylan frowned. He'd prepared to humiliate himself by groveling. "Who the heck am I talking to?" Whoever this guy was, it wasn't Chris Montgomery. It was his deep, gravelly, arrogant voice, but it sounded like the devil had mated with a unicorn, 'cause the shit coming out of his mouth was freaking rainbow-colored.

Down the line, a voice murmured in the background.

Ah, that explained it. The devil just got laid.

Well, applause to the fella for accomplishing the impossible and making Chris civil. "Keep that one you got there," Dylan said. He focused on Chris's mansion through the trees. Stately, impressive, and isolated. "Sounds like he might make a man out of you."

"Halsworth," Chris said, the sour detectable despite his

joyous intonation, "always such a riot. Of course you and the kids are welcome here. My place doesn't blow over at the wolf's first puff. It's brick. I take good care of all my property."

Poor little piggy. Dylan detected the unspoken snark and shoved his middle finger at the phone.

But snapping back wouldn't serve him. The bastard was doing him a favor, even if it stank of ulterior motive.

Dylan grinned at the sudden image of thirty kids running loose in that bachelor-pad mansion.

This might even be fun. "See you at five-thirty then," Dylan said.

"Wait—what? Five-thirty tomorrow evening, right?"

"Breakfast is at six."

A long silence stretched a bigger grin from him.

Chris said finally, "You know how much I love rising early to help out a troubled neighbor."

Dylan choked on a snort. The man never woke up before ten if he could help it. "Good stuff. See you bright and early, sunshine."

Chris laughed. The lack of response and the sudden dead tone of the phone was the "fuck you, Halsworth" Dylan had expected.

Until morning then . . .

Chapter Four

CHRIS

WHAT THE HELL was that sound?

Had Alexander left his cell phone behind? What kind of sick time was this to set an alarm?

Chris grabbed the pillow beside him and smashed it over his head. Shrill sound better stop soon. Couldn't even be six a.m. yet—

Shit!

He leaped out of bed and tripped over the sheets cuffing his ankles.

Hopping free with a stubbed toe, he shoved last night's tight jeans on.

The doorbell buzzed again. What a God-awful sound.

He imagined the glee Dylan felt ringing it like it was merry fucking Christmas.

His crumpled T-shirt smelled of someone else's aftershave, but no time to be picky. That bell was driving him insane.

Stomping into the foyer, he rubbed the sleep out of his eyes and yanked the door open. Should he slam it in Dylan's face? Maybe he didn't care if he was likeable after all.

Grinning, fresh-eyed Dylan studied Chris like he expected him to renege on his deal. "Looking great, sunshine."

"Fuck you, too."

Dylan stepped onto the threshold, his familiar woodsy-cinnamon scent breezing around Chris. "Better clog that potty mouth of yours, Montgomery. Kids'll be here soon."

Behind Dylan, two women wearing bright blue caps hauled boxes of food.

"Going to welcome us in?" Dylan's lips quirked. "Or do you need time to find your voice? Maybe you're waiting for your date to leave first?"

"No date, just me." He begrudgingly moved aside. "How the heck do you clog *your* potty mouth, Halsworth?"

Dylan folded his arms, stretching his bright blue T-shirt over a defined chest. If Chris didn't know better, he'd think the guy was posturing.

"Substitution. Don't think you'd be confident enough for it."

Chris hooked Dylan's firm bicep and pulled him out of the women's way. "Kitchen's through the foyer, down the hall, last room on the right." He pinched Dylan through his soft sleeve and let go. "I am f—*reaking* confident enough."

Dylan grinned. "Well, snickerdoodles. Fancy that." Snapping his boots over the polished marble floors, he hiked toward the kitchen.

Snickerdoodles?

Chris groaned and charged into the kitchen after him. If a bunch of hooligans was going to trample through his house, they needed ground rules.

"I want the kids supervised at all times. No touching anything unless I say it's okay."

Dylan entered the large kitchen that Chris barely used. It was too big for him. Besides, eating out was easier; he didn't have to cook or clean up after himself.

"This is perfect." Dylan threw him what possibly passed for a grateful smile. "The kids will be great. You'll love them."

Him? Kids? Uh, yeah—*hardly*.

Dylan continued, "This kid Jason reminds me of you at fourteen."

Chris blinked. When they were fourteen . . .

They'd been friends then. The best of. "He's a right pain-in-the-ass?"

Dylan smirked before focusing on the loads of cereal boxes and bread. "That would be correct if he was like you *now*."

CHRIS FOUGHT THE URGE TO DOZE, AND GOT TO BOILING EGGS.

He tensed at the stampeding feet, yelling, and something akin to laughter. At six in the morning, it didn't make any sense. The shiny kettle reflected his tousled, sleep-deprived appearance, so he ran a hand through his hair.

Dylan caught the move, and Chris wrenched his hand down. "I look like snickerdoodles."

"I love snickerdoodles," some kid said, as a group of adolescents swarmed into the dining room.

"Grab a bowl of cereal, eat, wash your plate," Dylan said.

Chris waited for the kids to finish breakfast before daring to squeeze into a spot at his dining table. He grabbed a boiled egg from the basket and cracked it open. Hard-boiled, all right. Looked green.

Across from him, Dylan raised a daring brow.

Chris ate it.

Conversation waxed and waned, littered with so many

"likes" Chris was cringing. Surely he'd never sounded so stupid as a kid?

Then again . . .

Okay, the kids could keep their "likes."

"I'm telling you, like, it totally works," said a lanky boy with fashionably messy hair, who lounged in his chair swirling a spoon in the air.

"No way, Jason."

This was the boy that reminded Dylan of his fourteen-year-old self?

Jason jabbed his spoon. "Yes, way." He leaned in conspiratorially, looking to Dylan and the dudes on either side of him. "Five hundred kisses is all it takes."

"Takes to what?" Dylan stole into the conversation with a quizzical look, pinching a piece of toast.

"To steal someone's heart. Anyone's heart."

Chris snorted. "No way. If you're not interested, you never will be."

"I'd trust him on this, Jason," Dylan said smoothly and snatched Chris's gaze. "He'd know."

Chris glared. "Right, I would know."

Dylan flushed. He stuffed the toast in his mouth and diverted his gaze.

"I could be kissed till the cows came home," Chris promised, "and never feel a thing."

Jason swung his spoon as he shook his head. "My brother did it with Chelsea—she hated his guts. Now they're all lovey-dovey and crap. Been going steady, like, a whole month now."

He pushed his chair out, and the dudes next to him followed. "Five hundred kisses is all it takes."

Chapter Five

DYLAN

"IT COULD BE true," Dylan said, regretting his decision to stay and clean. He should have dived in a boat and rowed back to camp with the kids. Outlining a three-week plan could be done by phone. Better yet, e-mail.

"No, it's not."

Dylan wrung out the washcloth with abandon before scrubbing the counters. Milk, cereal, and crumbs everywhere. "Have you ever actually let the same guy kiss you five hundred times?"

Chris wiped the adjacent counter. Snorted. "God, no."

"So you could be wrong."

Chris paused, cloth frozen in a puddle of milk. He leaned against the countertop. "Nope. No way am I wrong."

Dylan rolled his eyes and wiped down the counter Chris had neglected. "You're damn stubborn, Montgomery, you know that? Do you ever let anyone win besides yourself?"

"Hey, who generously gave up his place at five-thirty in the *freaking* morning and let kids rampage his kitchen!" A cocky smirk twitched Chris's mouth.

"You're working an angle with that."

"Maybe I want to be nice."

Dylan stalled at the slightest hitch in Chris's voice. Sincerity?

Probably not.

He approached Chris slowly. Any flash of real emotion vanished. God, that cocky curve of Chris's lips riled him. "Prove it."

"Prove it?"

"Prove you're right and Jason is wrong." Dylan touched Chris's chest, over his heart. "Five hundred kisses with the same guy." He chuckled, drily. "I pity the fool who has to suffer it. But anything in the pursuit of truth, right?" He leaned in, lowering his voice. "Unless you admit you could be wrong?"

Chris eyed Dylan's finger lazily drawing X's. "I—I'm not wrong." He cleared his throat. "You believe five hundred kisses can steal a heart?"

Hardly. But it would be impossible for Chris to follow through, and Dylan loved the idea of him giving up. For once not being so damn stubborn . . . "Sure."

Chris fisted Dylan's T-shirt and hauled him close. Firm lips planted hard against his mouth; teeth pulled open his bottom lip, tongue swept against his. Dylan's breath caught, surprise sweeping through his body to his feet.

Chris pulled back an inch. "One," he whispered over Dylan's chin. "Nothing. Didn't feel a thing."

Chapter Six

CHRIS

CHRIS'S LIPS TINGLED from the short, sharp kiss. He'd done it on impulse, to wipe the smug satisfaction off Dylan's face.

Dylan stood frozen, speechless.

Grinning, Chris kissed him again. "Two."

Dylan leapt back like someone had struck him with a thousand volts. "What the ever-living—?"

"Fuck? The kids are gone. You're safe." Chris crossed his ankles and plunged his hands into his pockets. "You wanted me to prove it."

"Not with *me*."

Dylan squirmed. Exactly the response Chris wanted. *Two can play at this game.*

He tamped down a laugh. "Not with you? Scared you'll fall for me?"

A furrowed brow, glowering eyes, and—

Dylan's body hit his—hard, warm—and those soft lips attacked. "Four. Five. Six."

"You miscounted."

"Seven. Making up for the one you've clearly forgotten."

Chris stiffened, and a soft, melancholic tickle worked through his veins.

He swallowed the memory and shoved Dylan off him at kiss number eight. "So you want me, huh?"

"Montgomery?" Nine. "Stop goading." Ten. "If you want out, admit you could be wrong."

"Not wrong. Just dreading the next four-hundred-and-ninety kisses."

Dylan's brow kicked up quizzically. "You know what to say to end this now."

Damn Dylan. Damn himself for being so stubborn.

Lips to Dylan's jaw, Chris nibbled a playful path to Dylan's ear, "You'd like that, wouldn't you?"

Chapter Seven

DYLAN

FEWER THAN TWELVE hours later, Dylan slumped onto his couch and cursed into the cushions. Did he have *screwed* stamped all over him? Both contracting companies estimated a month's worth of repairs. Three weeks if he paid a heck-of-a-lot more. Which he didn't have.

He complained again, hot breath bouncing off the pillow onto his neck.

Yells and laughs of kids—hanging out during free-activity time before dinner—rang in the distance.

Dinner.

The time tick-tocked toward six. Too quickly. Chris would be there—again—with his snarky comments, hard smile, and aggressive lean.

He wasn't ready to see him yet. He'd been secretly thankful Jeff had taken responsibility for lunch so he could hide behind the task of employing contractors and calling his dad, who was at a recovery spa in Hawaii. It meant he could pretend those kisses hadn't happened—wouldn't happen again.

With a groan, he rolled off the couch. His annoyingly small, one-person-wide kitchen was the reason he couldn't run meals from his own home. He cracked open a cold Mountain Dew.

It didn't taste as crisp and delicious as it usually did.

It tasted like agitation and reluctance. He wanted to stay at home for a month and not bother with Chris again. He could do it, too. Jeff could assume his tasks.

But . . .

He gulped half the can of Mountain Dew until his eyes watered and the back of his nose itched.

Not dealing with Chris would make it seem like he was avoiding him. Chris—damn him—would assume he had a point about Dylan falling for him.

Tossing the can in the trash, he decided he'd go to dinner and show how little he cared for Chris and his kisses.

Chapter Eight

CHRIS

Town busybody Mary Kindred walked through Chris's door with a large pot and an even larger smile.

"Mary," he said, welcoming her in.

"Where's the kitchen?"

"This way. Say, look," he said as he led her toward the kitchen, "the lease on Bennington Way is up for renewal soon?"

She looked sideways at him. "You waste no time."

He took the pot from her and settled it on the stove. "Should I turn it on?"

"Low."

He did as he was told and faced her, arms crossed, leaning against the counter. "I want to keep it."

Mary's expression flickered in surprise. She narrowed her eyes. "Really? You don't use the place."

True. He'd been through the woods nearly every month,

but only to look at his old cabin and reminisce. "Can I buy it off you? Make you a really good deal?"

"I'm not after money, Mr. Montgomery. The hiking club wants to extend their tracks, and that could lead to more visitors in town. It's a lovely piece of land. Seems a waste not to use it."

"I use it."

Mary raised a disbelieving brow. She lifted the lid off the pot and stirred with a large wooden spoon.

Chris tried again. Letting out a slow breath, he said, "It has sentimental value."

She paused mid-stir. "Sentimental," she repeated. "Your parents?"

Partly, yes . . . "Is there any way you'd renew my lease?"

She sighed. "I don't want to be cruel, you know, but I want to be sure if I did that—"

"Thank you."

"I said *if*. You'd need to care for the plot, and more than that, you'd need to get more involved in our community."

"I've never stopped hikers trekking through Bennington Way before."

"More involved than that, and I don't mean throwing money at things—time and effort, that's what this town needs. What I care about."

Chris nodded, hope catching in his throat. Time and effort? Sure. Anything.

Bennington Way had to stay with him.

Chapter Nine

DYLAN

DYLAN FORCED A slow, steady gait up the path to Chris's. Wafts of rosemary potatoes and stewed beef hit his nose as he followed the not-too-distant chatter of kids into the kitchen.

Mary commanded the room with no-nonsense rules, a chef's hat, and a warm grin. Dinner was always delicious when she was on duty. Employing her to moonlight for Wednesday dinners was the best move he ever made. Pity she had a day job. Not that he could afford to employ her full time. Besides, the locals would hate him. She ran Inglewood's local café, selling her famous scones and self-roasted coffee beans; she knew everything from street development and town-ball theme to who was having affairs with whom.

She ladled stew into thirteen-year-old starlet Holly's bowl and glanced at him. She gave a cheeky waggle-brow. "Looking good, handsome," she said with a cackle. "Goin' against camp colors tonight? Special occasion that I don't know about?"

The fridge door closed behind Mary and revealed Chris in loose jeans, an open shirt showing off his white tank top. He snapped open a Mountain Dew, brows arched, teasing. "I wonder what that special occasion could be?" He paused as he brushed past Dylan, whispering, "Good try, Halsworth. Won't work on me."

Wait. *What?*

Dylan hadn't dressed up. He wore a pair of jeans and a black button-up, which he'd worn for the contractors, too. Maybe he should have changed into a camp T-shirt, but he just wanted the evening over with.

He focused on Mary. "I can assure you there's nothing special about what I'll be doing tonight."

A snort made its way from the back of the room. "You won't be *doing* anything."

Chris's smirk faded as he stared at the thirty-odd faces between them. He blushed—honest-to-God blushed—and stammered, "Because we have other plans, remember?"

Mary shook her head and poured a bowl of stew and potatoes. "This one's for Mr. Montgomery." She loaded up a second bowl. "This one's yours. Want you well-fed, not powering yourself on sugary filth."

"Mountain Dew isn't sugary—"

Mary stopped him with a grimace. "I don't want to hear it."

Maybe she didn't, but that didn't stop Mountain Dew being his favorite pop ever since the mountain hiking trip his family and Chris's had taken when they were kids. Twelve-year-old Chris had been fun, adventurous—and, yes, sarcastic—but they'd been on the same team back then. Them against their folks. They smuggled pop into their hiking packs and drank it on the sly.

Chris once dared him to drink a can without stopping; his eyes had watered, and his throat had stung, but Dylan had done it, followed by a ripper-burp that got them and their elicit Mountain Dew caught.

The rest of that trip, the only mountain dew they experienced was the one that woke them with its cold morning grip.

Dylan sauntered toward the chorus of kids' conversations and snuck into a free chair next to Chris.

He set the steaming bowl and ice-cold pop can in front of him, stealing Chris's attention.

Did he also recall that trip? Or did a different memory play in his mind?

Maybe the one when they were sixteen, sitting on a ramp at the skatepark. Dylan had made Chris laugh mid-gulp, and he'd spat out a mouthful of pop in one misty cloud.

Chris startled to find Dylan watching him. He grabbed the can, took a long drink, and nudged the kid to his right. "What's this bet you guys are yapping about?"

The kid, Ryan, shook his head in disbelief. "You never heard of lantern night?"

Chris frowned. "Should I have?"

"Like, yeah."

Dylan cleared his throat. "Two teams pit against each other to make the best giant lantern."

Jason snagged Ryan's attention. "My team killed last year. Will this year, too."

"Whatever. Bring it on."

A shadow descended over Dylan's food. Mary glowered at them, pointing at their untouched stew. "You guys better eat that."

Dylan dug in while Chris flashed Mary a grin. "This is way too good to inhale," he said. "I want to savor your amazing cooking."

Chris delicately scooped up some beef. He chewed slowly, making delighted noises.

Mary rolled her eyes. "Schmoozing won't work, Mr. Montgomery. Next you'll be telling me you love kids."

Chris plastered on a smile. "But I do love kids. They're always welcome in my home."

Mary exchanged a knowing look with Dylan. *Who does he think he's fooling?*

Dylan set his spoon down. "So you wouldn't mind if we held a few camp events here? Our lantern-building contest? Your expansive backyard would be perfect."

Chris's smile widened, *thinned*. Dylan choked back a laugh.

"Absolutely." Chris inclined his head stiffly. "Go for it."

Mary clapped a tight hand on both their shoulders.

"That's the stuff I was talking about, Mr. Montgomery." She smiled. "I'm glad to see you and Mr. Halsworth working together again. It's been too long."

Dylan sighed. The evening was almost over.

Almost.

After three rounds of dinner, the kids and counselors had rowed back to camp, and Mary had finished packing her Chevrolet and left them with a wave out the window.

Nervously, Dylan shoved his hands into his pockets and followed Chris back into the mansion.

Hurry and finish. Prove you don't care about this.

In the kitchen, Dylan wiped the already clean table. Maybe he'd make number eleven long, hard, and deep. Make Chris give in, admit he could be wrong, end this challenge.

Chris sighed, and Dylan paused. Footsteps drew nearer . . .

Dylan scrubbed harder at invisible splotches.

Fingers brushed his ass, and Chris pulled Dylan's back pocket, urging him around.

He grabbed a handful of Dylan's shirt, and Dylan lurched into a bruising kiss. Their slick tongues eagerly invaded each other's mouths. Long, hard, deep.

A ravishing kiss . . . like Chris had the same idea. Dylan grinned into it.

A game of wills it was.

Changing tactics, Chris slowed the pace, leisurely exploring his mouth. Dylan slid a hand up Chris's arm and squeezed his nape, drawing him in tighter. Lips locked as he pushed Chris against the wall. Chests pinned together, Dylan drew back an inch and studied Chris's face.

Light played over his profile, glowing over swollen lips and flushed cheeks. Hard brown eyes held his stubbornly. *I won't give up first.*

"Eleven," Dylan murmured.

Chris cocked his head. "How many are we doing tonight?"

"As many as you can handle."

"I can handle anything."

"That right, Chris?"

Chris's throat worked, and he scowled. "Don't underestimate me."

"I'm well aware of what you're capable of."

Chris stiffened under him, eyes flashing like he'd been hit with a hundred memories. What did they look like from his perspective?

"Chris—"

"When's your kitchen fixed?"

Dylan sighed. "Not until the end of summer camp."

"Will the kids really be here for daily activities?"

A dry laugh shot out of him. "I can always tell Mary you can't stand them after all . . ."

"Bastard."

Dylan leaned in. Lowered his voice. "You know what to say to be left alone."

Chris shoved Dylan back against the wall, knocking the breath from him. The kiss whispered at his lip and dragged over his jaw to below his ear. "Twelve."

Shivers cascaded through Dylan and he moaned.

Chris pulled away, grinning.

Chapter Ten

CHRIS

A WEEK PASSED.

Rough, hurried, long, deep, strong, soft, languid, heated. Fifty-three more kisses; none of them meant anything, and each one was . . .

Chris stalked toward the boat shed, like he did every night after Dylan disappeared in his rowboat and clumsily splashed his way back to camp.

Stupid kisses.

Stupid competition.

Stupid stubbornness.

It bothered him that Dylan wouldn't give up.

Bothered him more that *he* wouldn't. Why did he love the torture so much? Why did he damn well dream of those lips and that body pressed against his?

The challenge in it.

If it had been anyone else, he might have dismissed it. Whatever. But because it was Halsworth . . . he had to press on until the end.

To think they'd ever been best friends.

Chris glared across the moonlit water. He'd never understand why he'd snuck over there as a kid.

Back then, he'd thought Dylan would never hurt him.

He hadn't believed he'd sabotage the boat Chris had worked on every Sunday for a year.

Never believed that when his parents died, Dylan wouldn't be there. He was supposed to know Chris needed him, even if they hadn't spoken for three years. He was supposed to *know* . . .

Chris stopped moving, throat tight, fists clenched in his pockets. "Shit." He craned his head toward the brightly starlit sky.

Every now and then, that loss swept over him, painfully rooting him to the spot.

He ripped himself toward his boat shed, shoving back the memories.

Wind rustled through the leaves of a nearby weeping willow, crickets sang, and—

Was that the sound of hushed whispers coming from his shed?

Yanking open the door, he called out. "Who's in here?"

"Oh, shit!" came a familiar young voice.

Chris switched on the light. There, in his unfinished boat, were Jason and Holly. Flushed faces and rumpled shirts explained the situation perfectly. Kids sneaking out of camp to make out.

"Out of the boat," he ordered.

They hurriedly complied. Jason muttered an apology to Holly under his breath.

"How'd you get here?" Chris asked, herding the two out of his shed.

"We rowed in the dinghy."

"Then that's the way we'll go back."

Chapter Eleven

DYLAN

"YEAH, YEAH, JUST a sec." Dylan hurriedly stepped out of the shower and wrapped a towel around his waist. The pounding at his door continued.

A counselor emergency? Hopefully nothing serious.

He dripped his way to the front door, checked the peephole, groaned, and opened. Chris.

"Keep your kids under control, Halsworth. I don't want them on my property after dark."

Dylan peered over Chris's shoulder. No kids to be seen. "What are you talking about?"

"Jason and Holly were having a make-out session in my boat."

"Where are they now?"

"Bumped into Jeff. He sent them back to their cabins."

"Ah, crap." This didn't look good for his security. Of course, sneaking out happened occasionally. He'd set extra supervision on the cabins. "Look," he said, running a hand through his wet hair, "I'm sorry about that. I can assure you, it won't happen again."

Chris pushed his way inside. "It'd better not."

Dylan stared after him. He hesitated, then shut the door.

"It was awkward." Chris scanned the modest living room and settled his gaze on him.

Suddenly the towel felt too small, too thin, too everything.

Chris blinked and turned sharply, heading for the kitchen.

Leaving the guy to his own devices, Dylan grabbed fresh clothes. He shoved on a pair of jeans and a linen shirt. Barefoot, he trod back to the living room.

With a can of Mountain Dew in each hand, Chris lounged on his couch.

"Here," Chris said, handing a can to him.

The pop cooled his fingers, his throat even more. Were they both studiously drinking to avoid conversation?

He should break the silence.

But say what?

Chris beat him to it. "What's on?" Picking up the remote, he switched on the TV. Baseball. Pirates against the Twins.

This was awkward. The last time Chris had hung at his place, they were sixteen and shared easy banter and disgusting jokes. Sometimes they spiked their drinks with vodka—

Sounded good about now.

He grabbed some from the freezer along with glasses.

The Twins played. They drank. They shot the shit about anything unrelated to them. Sports. Cars. Camping equipment. More sports.

"Safe, dammit. Clearly fucking safe!" Chris poured himself another vodka mix.

Dylan drained his glass and set it beside Chris's for a refill. "If we drank for every bad call, we'd be as drunk as that time in your cabin."

That night had launched them very close to the end of their friendship.

"Worst hangover of my life," Chris mused. "Dad blew a fuse when I came home. I think I was still drunk."

Dylan chuckled, but the humor quickly drained away. Late Mr. Montgomery had been strict, but he'd been a great dad. Always welcoming and accepting. When Chris came out, he had two parents who nodded and embraced him. Dylan still choked up remembering . . .

He missed the Montgomerys.

Taking the glass Chris held out for him, he swallowed. "When was the last time you visited the cabin? It's known as the haunted cabin around here. Every summer the kids ask me if I'll take them to see it." Every summer, he said no.

Too many memories.

That, and—even if most of the public hiked through it—Chris leased the land.

Chris shrugged. "A while ago."

They finished their drinks as the Twins entered the last inning. Dylan set his glass down.

Cling. Another glass met his on the coffee table. Chris's hand brushed his. An alcohol-induced zing rolled through him, like riding the surf.

They froze, and then Chris leaned in and kissed him. He tasted sweet and sticky. Aftershave lingered faintly on his skin. Dylan breathed it in sharply, and the kiss intensified.

Sixty-six. Sixty-seven. Sixty-eight. . . . Seventy.

When they broke, Dylan was on his back, Chris a warm, solid weight on top of him. Their gazes clashed as they caught their breath, and that smug grin returned.

"Nope," Chris said. "Still nothing."

Chapter Twelve

CHRIS

CHRIS WAS exhausted. Kids were hard work. Once this summer ended, he'd avoid them the rest of his life.

Okay, so maybe they cracked him up and said stupidly endearing things from time to time. But still, he would avoid . . .

Well, if Dylan was *really* hard up for help, he *might* offer to assist. But only for emergencies. Despite whatever the rest of town thought of him, he wasn't totally cold-hearted.

Chris tossed a baseball up and caught it. Across the field, Jason was readying his bat. The kid was a grade A smartass, and Chris liked him more for it.

Was this how Dylan remembered him as a kid?

Full of charisma and fun?

He smirked and pitched the ball. Jason swung. The bat hit the ball with an echoing *thwack*, and it was out of here. He dropped the bat and high-fived Ryan behind him.

Slowly, deliberately—and full of charisma, fun, and arrogance—he jogged his home run.

Chris gave the boy a lift of his cap in a show of respect.

Jason inclined his head in acknowledgment.

Maybe, just maybe—if Dylan *really* needed it—he could offer to run a few baseball games.

Chapter Thirteen

DYLAN

DYLAN ATE ANOTHER spoonful of pudding. Across from him, Jason and Chris were arguing about which baseball teams would make it to the playoffs.

"Hardly, not with a pitcher like that."

"Think the Twins will make it in this year?"

"Please."

Chris was laid back and genuinely engaged. It suited him, having kids around. Mellowed out his smugness.

Chris scraped the rest of the pudding from his bowl and licked his spoon. "What are you smiling at, Halsworth?"

Dylan's smile widened. "Nothing. It's a good day, is all." Especially since the workers repairing his kitchen said they might finish earlier than expected. "Maybe I'll tell you later."

Later happened once the kids had cleared out, and Chris had backed him into a wall. A kiss tickled his bottom lip, and Dylan ran his teeth over the tingle to stop it.

"Now, tell me," Chris said, inching toward kiss one-hundred-and-eighteen. "What has you in such a pleasant mood?"

One-hundred-and-nineteen. One-hundred-and-twenty. "We'll be out of your hair in a week. Contractors will finish early."

Dylan expected a whoop of joy and a horribly relieved smile, not a pregnant pause and a slow nod.

Chris pushed off the wall. "I mean, that's . . . great. Be good to have the place to myself again."

Chris and his bachelor-pad mansion. This big, echoing mansion.

Dylan pitied him.

"Better race through the rest of these damn kisses, then," Chris cleared the croak in his voice and resumed his cocky lean. "Sooner the better."

The next day, Dylan stood between Jeff and Chris, shaking his head at Jason and Ryan playing Twister on the colored grass. Five girls surrounded the two boys in a crescent moon. Holly stood grinning at the board, spinning the arrow.

He and Chris weren't the only ones who couldn't say no to a challenge.

"Come on," Jason said as Ryan shoved his leg to red, knocking his ear. "We can handle your bet, Hols. But can you girls handle ours?"

Holly spun the arrow. "Left hand blue."

Jason and Ryan crashed to the spray-painted grass. *Chris's* grass. But the guy had taken it better than Dylan expected. He'd barely blinked when he learned the kids had defaced his backyard with red, green, yellow, and blue spots.

Jason picked himself out of the tangle and helped Ryan up.

He slung an arm around his friend's shoulder and nicked his head at Holly. "Me and my buddy dare you girls to listen to our retelling of 'Red Ribbon.'"

Holly snickered. "Think we're scared of a stupid ghost story?"

A smirk twitched Jason's lips. "You will be." Turning, the boy snatched Jeff's gaze. "Did you ask about camping at the haunted cabin?"

Jeff shoved his hands in his pockets and faced Dylan.

Here it comes, just like every year.

"Well, you heard him," Jeff said with a shrug, "should we set something up?"

"Spook night. Spook night. Spook night," Jason and Ryan chanted, fists pumping above their heads.

Dylan shook his head, and stopped at Chris's arched brow.

"Why not? What camp doesn't run a horror night for the older kids?"

Camp Halsworth.

The chanting grew into a chorus as the girls joined. Even Jeff was tapping his foot along with the beat.

Dylan took Chris out of earshot from Jeff and the kids. "The haunted cabin is yours—"

Chris snorted and gestured around them. "Mine? Like that's stopped you."

Dylan fished for another excuse to keep away from the cabin—*those memories*. "I don't have enough counselors to take the eldest out camping for the night."

"If you're that desperate," Chris said, shuffling from foot to foot. "I could come with you."

Dylan blinked. "Are you volunteering to help us?"

Chris shifted suddenly. "Don't get the wrong idea, Halsworth. It's a prime opportunity to scare the bejesus out of you."

Jason appeared out of nowhere, ramming against his side

with a hoot of laughter. "Yeah, scare the girls *and* Mr. Halsworth. This'll be epic."

"Scare me?" Dylan readjusted his Camp Halsworth cap. "I've lived my whole life around campfire stories. I ain't been scared yet."

Scanning the hopeful, chanting chorus of kids behind them, he gave in. "Fine," he called out to them, effectively silencing the crowd. "Friday we camp at the haunted cabin. Bring it."

Chris nodded toward the mansion. "Could I see you in private for a second, Mr. Halsworth? To discuss scary details?"

Inside, Chris shut the door and shoved Dylan against the cool, hard wood. Chris leaned against him. Length to length. Nose to nose.

"One-hundred-and-thirty-one." Chris hovered toward a kiss. Dylan grabbed the lapels of Chris's shirt, pulling him that last half-inch to his mouth. Slightly chapped lips and rough stubble moved over his mouth and chin. Their tongues met in a hurried clash, and Chris pressed harder against him.

Dylan drew his hands to the back of his neck. With a fistful of short hair, he pulled. Chris answered with another thrust of his tongue.

"Yep," Dylan murmured when they took a second to catch a breath. "Those are some scary details."

A grin stretched Chris's lips, and his eyes lit with amusement.

Dylan grinned back.

They broke apart. Chris ran a hand through his hair and hooked his thumbs in the waistband of his shorts.

Dylan slowly peeled himself off the door. "Guess we should . . ." He gestured toward the backyard.

"Yeah," Chris agreed. "Yeah."

Chapter Fourteen

CHRIS

CHRIS COULD TELL his story had creeped Dylan out by the startled jump he gave when the fire crackled, and then again when a twig snapped behind the decrepit-looking cabin.

Holding his smirk in check, Chris encouraged Jason to tell his story. Between him and the other counselors—Jeff, Dylan, and Heather—ten girls and boys huddled under woolen blankets. Holly kept laughing off the boy's story, but her laugh grew strained. She and some of the others—boys included—kept eyeing the tents, as if they wished they could crawl into them and end the horror.

Of course, no one wanted to leave the group alone.

". . . the red ribbon curled around the girl's neck, softly at first, so she thought it was magical, something good. She heard a whisper, telling her to walk into the woods, where more magic awaited her. All she had to do was step inside the haunted cabin and let out the ghost of Mr. Ripple. A sad, lonely man, who'd died alone . . ."

Susan shivered violently next to him, and Chris took pity on her. "It's just a story." When her teeth started chattering, he added, "I know for a fact that cabin is not haunted."

"H-how do you know?" she asked him quietly.

He fished in his pocket for keys. "Because it's mine. I used to hang out here on weekends, with Dy—" He swallowed. "It only looks scary because I haven't taken care of it."

"Why not?"

He shrugged. "Grew out of it." *Didn't have anyone to hang out here with anymore.*

Looking over the fire, he found Dylan watching him. Chris clasped the keys in his fist and stuffed them back into his pocket.

". . . each step the girl took, the ribbon shifted around her neck, comfortable, lulling . . . Then in the middle of the woods, where no one but her friends could hear her thrash about, where no one could help her, the ribbon tightened, and tightened, and tightened . . ."

Holly screamed when Jason snuck a hand to her nape and squeezed. Once she'd recovered, she glowered at a giggling Jason. "Just you wait," she threatened, before the counselors broke up the storytelling and sent the girls and boys into their separate tents.

Chris sat alone on his log. How had he so easily offered to camp out here, when he'd not been able to force himself for years?

He'd done it spontaneously. Without real thought.

Like that first—second—kiss with Dylan.

The fire fizzled to glowing embers, and the chatter of kids in their tents died down. Something moved beside him, and he turned expecting to see Dylan—

A large garden spider scuttled over the log.

Chris leaped up and over the ember pit, coming to a screeching halt in front of a quietly conversing Dylan and Jeff.

Dylan raised a brow. "You good there, Montgomery?"

Chris squared his shoulders. "Sure thing. Just off to my tent. Night."

Jeff wished him a good sleep.

Dylan donned a knowing smirk and glanced pointedly toward the log Chris had abandoned.

"Whatever," he said, and passed them.

Dylan watched him over his shoulder, and while Jeff was facing away, Chris kissed his middle finger and blew it over to Dylan.

Chapter Fifteen

DYLAN

Dylan shook Jeff three times, hoping to suffocate the snoring. The guy slept like a log truck over a gravel road, loud and solid.

He wriggled out of his sleeping bag, threw it over his arm, and snuck out of the two-man tent into the night. Save a whistling wind and Jeff's snores, the camp was quiet.

Crunching over grass and wilted leaves, he made for Chris's tent. A foot away there came a shuffling and a *ziiiiiip*.

Chris popped his head out of the tent and rolled his eyes. "Thought I heard you." He ducked back into the double tent and Dylan snuck in after him.

"Jeff snores like you wouldn't believe," Dylan said, hunched in the small space.

Chris scooted back into his sleeping bag, laughing. "I can hear it from here."

"Up close it vibrates." He dumped his sleeping bag on the

ground. He couldn't crash with Heather. This was his only option. "I'm setting up next to you in here."

A rather loud snort came in answer. "How about no."

Dylan sank to his knees on his feather-down sleeping bag. No way was he heading back to Snoreville. "You afraid something might happen?" He jerked his thumb toward the rest of camp. "'Cause I got about a dozen reasons why it won't. The tippy-top of which being—*hell no*."

Chris laughed. "Dude, that isn't the issue."

"Why not?"

Milky moonlight filtered through the open tent flap, showcasing the evil grin that twisted Chris's lips. "I like watching you suffer." Chris shifted into his sleeping bag and rested on his side, head propped up on his hand. "My sadist side will be satisfied if you admit to being scared *snickerdoodle-less* by my story."

Dylan rested his pillow at the top of his sleeping bag. "I was *not*—"

Chris snatched his pillow and stuffed it behind him. "You want a place to sleep or not?"

"You're cruel, Montgomery."

"Yeah, but you'll get me back for it."

They both grinned.

"Fine," Dylan said, gesturing for his pillow back. "I got creeped out by your story. Good enough?"

"Hmm, not really. But I take pity on you." He threw the pillow, and Dylan caught it against his chest. "Don't ever say I'm not compassionate."

"Bastard." Dylan climbed into the sleeping bag, turning away from the man.

Their quiet breathing was more distracting than Jeff's snores. Dylan's whole body was tense as he tried to convince himself not to think of the man behind him or count his breaths to check if they were as unsteady as his own. After half an hour, he clenched his jaw and twisted to his other side—

Chris was watching him. Their gazes clashed, and Chris raised an audacious brow.

Under his breath, Dylan let out an uncensored curse and leaned in to kiss him. Once. Hard and brief. Full of frustration. Frustration from not sleeping. Nothing else.

Absolutely not.

He jerked back a couple of feet and slammed his head back down on the pillow. Chris's grin mocked him. "Not even tolerable in the dark."

Chapter Sixteen

CHRIS

THREE HOURS LATER, tossing and turning, Chris gave up on sleep. Dylan was too warm, too close. Chris wanted to roll toward him, nuzzle closer.

He glared at the tent ceiling.

He needed to walk.

Quietly, keys in hand, he slipped out of the tent.

Moonlight sparkled over the cabin, turning it ghostly white. A breeze whistled from it, beckoning him closer. Holding his breath, Chris snuck up to it. Wooden porch planks groaned under his feet, and the door felt cold under his fingertips. The door handle willed him to clasp it and enter the past once more.

Chris shut his eyes and rested his forehead against the softening wood.

"Fuuuuuck."

"Chris?"

Chris spun around. Dylan stood three feet away, face pensive.

Panic shot through Chris. He shook his head hard and hoofed past Dylan. "Nothing. This means nothing."

Dylan pulled him close. "I don't believe you." The words fluttered over Chris's lips. Heart hammering against his chest, Chris shook his head, but Dylan cupped the back of his neck and drew him into a kiss.

Chris melted into it and ripped himself out. "One hundred and forty-four. Still nothing. There'll always be nothing."

He hurried back to his tent, jumped into his sleeping bag, and slammed his eyes shut. Dylan snuck in next to him, sighed, and—much later—drifted to sleep.

Morning found Chris rising at the first scuffle outside. "Time to get up."

A sleepy groan-turned-laugh rumbled out of Dylan. "That coming from you?"

"Yeah, funny. Let's get this show on the road. I have things to do."

And things to forget.

Chris finished the fiberglass covering and stepped back to admire his handiwork. It'd taken a few months, but he was close to finishing his mahogany runabout. He smiled, admiring the authentic-looking bow.

Next he had to install the motor and propeller shaft, and then deck the hull. He couldn't wait to take it out for a spin and show Dylan how to really drive a boat—

He frowned and forced himself to focus on cleaning up. Dylan didn't belong in this shed with his beautiful boat. Didn't belong anywhere in his life.

Fuck. He needed a break. Everywhere he turned, Dylan

was there. Kids were in his kitchen three times a day, or out in his yard. Nowhere could he escape the word Halsworth.

He took *Rosita*, his utility boat, motored around the lake to town and made the ten-minute walk to Luscious Café. He followed the sweet aroma of freshly baked raspberry white chocolate scones right to the counter. He resisted buying one and stuck to his usual latte.

"Having this here today?" Mary asked, gesturing toward his usual table in the cozy couch-filled room.

When in the last ten years had he done differently?

"Like every time." The small, sunshine-yellow table by the window offered the best view of the lake.

Mary's words followed him. "People change their minds sometimes."

She carried over his latte. "I had this guy who absolutely hated the smell of eggplant. Said he'd never in a million years try it." She rested her hands on her hips and grinned. "Well, he waltzed in here the other day, didn't he? Ordered the savory pie special. I didn't tell him there was eggplant in it, and he gobbles the thing up and orders seconds."

"I like this spot," Chris said and sipped his latte.

Mary sighed and retreated.

A heavy laugh cut across the room. Max, from the gym outside Grand Rapids. They'd flirted from time to time. They hadn't hooked up, but tension was brewing. "Max, what brings you here?"

Max squeezed into the adjacent seat. "Passing through. Haven't seen you at the gym for a while." He winked. "Actually, I have a day off. Was planning a hike, unless you want to grab a drink?"

Chris shifted uncomfortably, straining for a grin. He lifted his latte. "Already have one of those."

Max didn't waste time. He leaned in, pausing with his

mouth close to Chris's ear. "Not the kind of drink I was thinking of."

Setting his glass down, Chris shook his head.

A frown cut into Max's brow as he rested back in the chair. "You with someone, Montgomery?"

"No. Absolutely not. I . . . I have a bunch of kids back at camp. It's just not a good time."

"Right." Max stood. "Gotcha. Another time, then?"

Chris blinked and shrugged. "I mean . . . yeah, sure. Another time."

Max made a quick retreat.

His backside was firm, tight. His jeans were slung just right. But—

Fuck, he needed to hurry through these kisses with Dylan. The whole situation was screwing with his head. He barely tolerated the guy.

The coffee was murky, like his thoughts. Maybe he should admit to Dylan he was wrong. Jason and his 500-kiss theory *could* have merit. But would that sound like the contest was affecting him?

It wasn't.

He tipped the last of the coffee into his mouth and headed back to the register. He planted twenty bucks on the counter. "Two scones to go please. Keep the change."

Mary returned bluntly, "Keep up the good community work."

Chapter Seventeen

DYLAN

"TWO MORE DAYS, you think?" Dylan asked the foreman, who settled his yellow helmet back on his head.

"Yep. Then we'll be outta here."

Dylan could've hugged the guy. Life would soon return to its old status-quo.

Over the foreman's shoulder, through a gap in the trees, Chris's boat motored into view. An everyday sight, except that the boat was angled toward his property. Dylan took his leave and arrowed for the jetty.

Chris docked. A short clash of acknowledging gazes preceded his tying *Rosita* up. He leaped gracefully onto the jetty.

Chris's gait was confident. Steady. Dylan's skin prickled, and a shiver rippled through him.

He cleared his throat. "What brings you to Camp Halsworth?"

A foot from him, Chris lifted a paper bag. "Scored us some scones. Now I'm hoping to score something else."

Dylan laughed. "You're to the point."

He beckoned him to the bench he'd erected in memory of Chris's parents. It overlooked their favorite part of the lake.

Chris stared at the embossed bronze plate, Adam's apple jutting.

"We can sit somewhere else," Dylan said softly.

"Here's fine." Chris sank onto the bench, blinking rapidly. He dropped the paper bag between them.

The tension was heavy, taut—close to snapping.

Dylan peeked into the bag. "Mary's famous raspberry-and-white-chocolate scones. I could kiss you."

Chris stared intently at him, as if searching for something. An answer? The old Dylan who was once his best friend? "Kiss me," he croaked.

"What are you thinking, Chris?"

He bristled. "I want to get them out of the way."

"What's the hurry?"

Chris's smirk didn't fit him correctly. Too large. Too wobbly.

"What's the hurry? You dislike it as much as I do, right?"

Dylan paused, glanced across the glittering lake. "Right."

Chris handed him a scone. Crunchy on the outside, fluffy on the inside, chocolate baked to perfection, but Dylan couldn't enjoy it.

Chris wiped a loose crumb off Dylan's lips and followed it with a light kiss. "One-hundred-and-forty-five."

Dylan's skin prickled all over again. "Do you think about our first kiss?"

Chris laughed—high, tight. He rubbed his nape. "You do?"

"I was sixteen, it was my first kiss. Of course I do."

Chris broke a chunk off his scone and threw it into the lake, toward the lazily looping swans.

Dylan rested his forearms on his knees, staring into the distance. "One day there was the promise of your lips on mine, and then the next you were gone. Off courting your next conquest."

Chris crumbled the rest of his scone and dropped it into the water. "You were my friend."

"Exactly, I was your friend," Dylan said. Friends didn't abandon one another.

Chris looked toward his boat, as if regretting coming here. Typical Montgomery. Shrug off anything that was real. Anything that involved feelings.

"Whatever," Dylan muttered. "Leave if you can't handle this."

Chris turned in his direction, and Dylan swallowed his anger at the sheen in his eyes. "We were too young. It never would have worked. I didn't . . . didn't . . ."

"Didn't what? Like me like that? Your message was loud and clear when you stood me up at the cabin."

Dylan had snuck out of the house to meet him there at midnight, rose in hand. He waited, convincing himself Chris couldn't figure a way to sneak out. Dawn came and went. Dylan slumped home and dressed for school.

Chris didn't spare him a glance all day, and when Dylan went to confront him at the bike shed—

Well, the guy had his tongue down Joseph McHay's throat.

Dylan tossed the rest of his scone toward the swans.

Chris stumbled over his words. "What I meant was I didn't . . ."

"Care?" Dylan's shoulders slumped. "Spit it out, Chris."

Chris lurched to his feet. "I didn't want it not to work! Jesus, I thought if we waited . . . You wouldn't listen and then you keyed my boat. You knew how long I spent on that."

Glued to the bench, Dylan couldn't move, couldn't even speak.

He'd taken his key to the haunted cabin and, in a fit of hurt, marked up Chris's boat with MAN SLUT. His voice crackled. "That was . . . what I did was out of line. I never should have reacted like that."

Chris stumbled back a few steps. Again with the indifferent shrugging. "Yeah, well, whatever. It doesn't matter. We can take these kisses as slow as you like. I'll never feel anything for you."

With a dimpled smile that didn't reach his eyes, Chris boated out of there, leaving Dylan sitting on the bench amidst their crumbs.

Two days later, the construction work was completed. The last of the subcontractor's trucks made dust clouds down the gravel path as they zipped out of there. Dylan folded his arms, knowing he should feel more relieved that they were done.

He sighed and took in the dining hall, the repaired roof, new tiles bright against the older ones. One final inspection, and the kids could eat at camp again.

Dylan kicked at the gravel, sending it scuttling toward the lakeshore and the jetty.

Chris.

How he'd gazed at the wood and wrought iron, at the bronze plaque with his parents' names on it . . .

His stomach twisted. The last two days he'd avoided him, dwelling on all the ways Chris had hurt him. But he'd hurt Chris, too.

Staring over the lake to the edge of Chris's property, Dylan sighed and headed for his dinghy.

DYLAN FOUND CHRIS HAMMERING AT A LOOSE PLANK ON HIS jetty. He wore jeans and a tank top, and the sun beamed down on him, highlighting the sheen of sweat over his upper arms and brow. Dylan paused to watch him—

Chris glanced up over the water. Their gazes met for a second before Chris continued pounding away.

Jumping out of his dinghy, Dylan strode toward him. A dozen feet away, Chris dropped his hammer and stood, shoulders set hard as if expecting attack. "What do you want, Halsworth?"

Three feet, two, one—

Dylan wrapped his arms around the man's shoulders and hugged him.

Chris tensed in his grip, and Dylan spoke at his ear. "I was an ass. A complete ass to key your boat. I'm embarrassed, and I'm sorry."

Chris relaxed, resting in the embrace. It felt comfortable, holding the man like this. Dylan's stomach fluttered.

Breathing in a mix of sweat and aftershave, he squeezed Chris again on impulse. A soft puff of breath hit his neck in answer, and a shiver rolled through him.

He untangled them, and kissed Chris lightly on the mouth. No number. No commentary.

"Yeah, that's all."

Dylan retreated down the jetty.

A frown cut Chris's brow, and he traced his lips with the tip of his finger.

Dylan swallowed, jumped into his dinghy, and rowed home.

Chapter Eighteen

CHRIS

AFTER THE kids had cleared out and the dinner dishes were clean, Chris threaded his fingers with Dylan's and pulled him into the living room. He kissed Dylan at the door, and again at the couch. Flicking on the television, Chris kissed him some more.

He couldn't shake the shivery feeling Dylan had left him with on the jetty.

He'd been convinced Dylan would avoid coming over for dinner with the kids after that, but lo and behold, he'd been the first to arrive.

And, as was becoming habit, he'd been the last to leave.

Chris smiled and dropped to the couch. Dylan lounged next to him in his jeans and a blue Camp Halsworth T-shirt that'd hitched to reveal the red elastic of boxer-briefs.

"What're we watching?" Dylan peeked at him out the corner of his eye.

"Baseball. Should be on any minute now." In the meantime, since the commercials were so damn boring . . .

He leaned over, snagged a fistful of that blue T-shirt, and brought those soft lips once more to his. His hand curved around Dylan's back, and he dragged it slowly to that triangle of skin peeking out at the hip.

Dylan's breath hitched, and Chris wanted to make that happen again. It gave him goosebumps. Big, shivery goosebumps—

Dylan pulled away. "One thing, Montgomery."

Chris tensed. "Halsworth?"

"The inspector gave the dining hall the okay. The kids can eat back at camp."

"Oh." He fumbled with the buttons on the remote. He hated commercials, dammit. The numbers blurred, but he pressed anyway. "That's it? None of those rascals coming back over here?"

"You're a free man."

"Well, I . . . You know . . ." Fuck, his throat was tight. "They always said such ridiculous things."

Why can't I admit one true thing? Why can't I just say I'll miss the stomping, laughing, screaming . . .

Dylan clasped his hand around the remote, their fingers touching. "You okay? The kids will miss traipsing around this big house of yours."

Big and empty house, now.

Fuck.

He shrugged and stared at the screen. "I mean, I might miss them, too. A little."

Dylan turned on the sports channel. "We're still using your yard for lantern night this Friday. Mary is super excited about it."

Chris closed his eyes and nodded. Good. He could give the kids a proper goodbye on lantern night.

He stood, throat tight, eyes prickling. "Drink? I'm gonna grab some . . ."

He marched to the kitchen. The fridge opened with a squeal, and Chris lingered in the cool air, resting his head against the top frame, staring at the packs of pop.

He needed to get a grip.

He snapped two cans free, straightened his shoulders, and headed back to the lounge. To his ex-best-friend turning . . . friend again?

The lump in his throat tightened.

LANTERN NIGHT. TECHNICALLY, EVENING. THE SUN SETTLED warmly over his backyard. Sheets of taped cardboard stretched before him and the kids sitting on the dyed grass, carving out their designs.

Chris's team had decided on a dragon theme, and—*wow*.

He'd never seen such talented kids—the dragon cutout displayed a long snout, spanned wings, and a snaking tail.

He worked alongside Mary and Heather and a bunch of kids he barely knew the names of. Except for Jason and Holly and Tom and Carlo and Susan and—maybe he did know all their names.

Mary shoulder-bumped him. "What're you daydreaming about?"

He startled. "Nothing."

"You were smiling." She leaned in and whispered, "If I didn't know better, I'd think you love this." She gestured to the kids, the lantern mess, and Dylan—standing on the far side of the field—laughing and rubbing his hands together.

Chris shrugged.

Mary shook her head, smirking. "I like this Mr. Montgomery. I hope you keep it up after I renew your lease."

He whipped toward her. "Really?"

"Yes, really—"

Chris yanked her into a twirling hug that had her yelping and laughing.

"Stop the hugs," Jason screeched. "We need the cellophane, go, go, go!"

Holly tugged his sleeve as soon as he let Mary go. "Get there before we get left with baking paper!"

Chris followed his orders, racing to the end of the half-mile garden where the supplies were stacked.

Dylan ran toward the supplies on behalf of the other team. *Of course.*

These were the rules: counselors/adults fought for the limited materials, and kids were the only ones allowed to work with them.

Mary had won them the craft knives, leaving the rival team to use safety scissors and their hands.

Race time.

He accelerated into a sprint. Dylan sped up, too. They shared a determined glance and zoomed toward their prize. The cellophane sat between tinfoil and a box of string.

Kids chanted behind them, a chorus of "Montgomery" and "Halsworth."

Chris grinned. He was a foot ahead.

Dylan dove and slid into Chris's legs, crushing the box of cellophane.

"Fudge snickerdoodles! You *dove*?"

A hard chuckle, and Dylan hauled himself to his feet, arm hooked around the cellophane box. "Have fun with the baking paper, sunshine." He jogged off, calling over his shoulder, "I'll be back for the tape."

Not going to happen.

Grabbing the box filled with rolls of baking paper, he raced back, dumped it, and turned around again.

Dylan didn't run as fast as before.

"Worn out already, Halsworth?" Chris called out as he charged for the supplies.

"Giving you a chance to catch up, Montgomery. Beating you isn't as fun otherwise."

This time Chris dove. But not for the tape. He tackled Dylan around the waist, bringing him to the ground with a thump.

Dylan spat out a mouthful of dirt and grass. "Cheater."

Snagging the tape, Chris shook his head. "Not against the rules." He found the second-best option for the rival team. String. He dropped it at Dylan's nose. "There you go. Let's see who wins."

Laughing, Dylan climbed to his knees. They stared at one another for a few long seconds, and Chris's smile widened.

Dylan pulled his gaze away. "Till our next round," he said quietly.

Chris wasn't sure he was referring to the lantern-making competition.

CHRIS GRINNED AND MOVED TOWARD THE GLEAMING LANTERNS. Their team kicked ass. Dylan's had trouble stringing on their cellophane.

He laughed, butterflies in his belly dancing. God, he hadn't felt so elated in years.

Mary had agreed to renew his lease on Bennington Way, and—

The lease thing.

Counselors herded kids to the boats for curfew, and Dylan stayed behind. As always.

Chris glanced at the silhouette in front of the giant dragon-themed lantern. Orange-gold flickered behind Dylan as he waved to the rowing kids just before they slipped out of view.

Chris cut across the grass toward him. "You love cleaning up, don't you?"

The silhouette turned, and lantern light shimmered over Dylan's sharp nose, strong jaw, arching brow.

"What makes you think that?" came Dylan's gravelly, amused voice.

"Why else do you always volunteer to do it?"

"Someone has to."

"You could ask any of your employees."

Six inches away, Chris stopped.

Dylan looked out toward the shimmering navy lake. Copper strands in his dark hair glowed.

Chris's skin tingled and tension stretched between them, sudden and sharp. Dylan shifted, a gentle frown cutting his brow. His lips parted, poised to say something—

Nervousness bubbled in his belly and he snatched Dylan's words away with a kiss.

His tongue stole inside Dylan's mouth, twisting, seeking, exploring. They grabbed each other, groins surging forward.

Chris liquefied in those strong arms and sank deeper into the embrace.

The kiss grew fervent, hands seeking flesh under their shirts. Chris's skin sang. Kissing Dylan lighted every nerve ending.

Dylan gripped Chris's hair, dragging a moan from him. Their foreheads rested together as they caught their breath.

Dylan chuckled. "One-hundred-and-seventy-two."

That number pissed Chris off. It was an intruder. Didn't belong there.

He snagged Dylan into another kiss, and another: 173, 174, 175, 176 . . . languid kisses turned into hot, hard little nips on his lips and then over his jaw, down his neck. 188, 189, 190, 191, *more.*

He undid the buttons on Dylan's shirt, leaving kisses in their place. Dylan's neck tasted warm as he drew his hands under the soft fabric and pushed it off Dylan's shoulders.

His lips moved to Dylan's firm chest, pebbled with goose-bumps under his lips.

Reaching a nipple, he flicked out his tongue. A sharp intake of breath and a hand threading into the back of his hair had Chris sucking the nipple into his mouth.

Dylan moaned and Chris's cock strained against his jeans. He dropped slowly to his knees, kissing a path down past Dylan's navel.

He reached to the belt blocking his path—

What the fuck was he doing?

Why did he ache to continue? To take Dylan in his mouth and make him yell out his name.

Chris jerked back, rising hurriedly.

Oh Fuck.

He strode toward his house and didn't look back.

Chapter Nineteen

DYLAN

DYLAN SHOVED HIS shirt on. The door slammed shut just as he began jogging after Chris. Damn, Jeff had the spare key.

He rang the doorbell. Nothing. He pounded on the hard wood.

"Come on, Chris. Open up. We're not sixteen anymore. We have to talk about this."

A shuffle came from behind the door.

Dylan flattened his hand on the wood and leaned into it. "Please, let's talk."

Chris cracked his door open, the chain barring access. Brown eyes sheened, and the emotion in them punched into Dylan. "Chris . . ."

"You win, Halsworth. I give up. I'm wrong. Jason was right about the 500-kiss theory. Now, we're done. Game over. Goodbye."

"Wait—"

The door shut in his face. Dylan leaned his forehead against it, his breath bouncing off the wood back to him. "Please, open up."

A muffled sniff. "Just go."

Reluctantly, Dylan retreated.

He couldn't sleep.

Crack of dawn the next morning, Dylan rowed back to Chris. House key recovered from Jeff, he snuck inside. The foyer echoed his steps.

"Chris?" He beelined for Chris's bedroom, just like he'd done as a kid.

The walls had been repainted, but the massive bed stood in the same spot, with the same stunning view of the lake and Dylan's property.

Bedding was twisted and half draped off the bed. "Chris?" he called softly, inching to the bathroom.

No Chris.

The rest of the house held no sign of him either. Dylan stared at the kitchen counter where they'd started their surprising—life changing—kissing challenge. He closed his eyes and savored the tingle of that kiss.

Dylan found a pen and paper and hesitantly wrote. His heart slammed against his chest with each word and his stomach twisted. He read the sentence twice, three times, and then set it on the counter and walked out of the mansion.

Chapter Twenty

CHRIS

CHRIS MOTORED TO the jetty on the far side of Halsworth's property. Breathing in the warm, shady morning, he strolled to the picnic bench where he and Dylan had shared scones.

Frost glittered over the plaque with his parents' names and he used the cuff of his sleeve to wipe it off. Cold flakes bit into his palm and ran down his arm, numbing his skin but not the pain . . . not the hope . . .

Dylan had cared.

Chris sat on the bench. The lake rippled, and a breeze whispered around him.

He could almost still see them, sixteen, sitting in a leaky dingy in the lake, laughing even as they bucketed water out of the small boat.

Dylan had gasped when Chris threw the water at him;

Dylan returned the favor. An epic water fight in a rapidly sinking dingy.

Chris had lunged and they both fell overboard. They'd laughed so hard as they swam to shore, towing their boat by the rope. When they reached the jetty, they knotted the rope to the pylon and collapsed from the effort. Laughter tickled every inch of him, and that warm breeze added to it. Dylan pushed to his feet and offered Chris a hand.

Chris hauled Dylan back down with a smartass comment. Dylan toppled heavily atop him, chest to chest, groin to groin. Through their laughter, they stared at each other and the moment pulsed through Chris right to his groin.

Dylan's too. He'd felt it. Arched into it, flipped Dylan to the jetty, and pressed their lips together. His body roared. Their soft kiss deepened until Chris was sure Dylan would lose his virginity right then and there on the jetty, and as much as Chris had wanted to be that guy . . .

He'd pulled back and shook his head. "Not now. Not here."

Chris had pulled Dylan by the hand, standing awkwardly, still giggling, and they raced down the jetty and bombed into the lake. Dylan knotted their hands underwater once more. "Meet tonight? At the cabin?"

God, the memory ached.

Chris pressed his frosty sleeve against his forehead and cursed.

He sat on the bench for half an hour and moped into town. Mary smiled at him, and Chris drank his coffee in his corner. It tasted of routine and loneliness. Their first kiss played in his head, and he blinked hard. Leaving the coffee half drunk, Chris walked every inch of the town that held moments of the two of them. He started at the school, where they'd once climbed into the sprawling cherry tree to avoid a dog foaming at the mouth.

He peeked inside their old classroom. Pictured Dylan

lounging in the back trying to balance a ruler on his nose, or reading comics when he should have been studying. A thousand memories were held in that room, but the one that Chris felt the deepest was the one after their kiss.

The one where Dylan had tried to steal his attention, and Chris badly wanted to push him up against the bike shed but was so scared.

Chris stared into the empty classroom, head pressed against the cool glass. If he'd known that was the beginning of the end . . .

Chris turned on his heel and hoofed it back to his boat.

He read the note on the kitchen counter and hauled in an unsteady breath.

Meet tonight? At the cabin?

At dusk, Chris drove to the cabin, nervously tapping the steering wheel.

He parked his truck and saw Dylan sitting on the porch. Chris's throat closed up as he moved to meet him.

They stood close to the spot they'd last shared a tent.

He fidgeted with his keys, and then—with faux confidence—charged past Dylan to the cabin. Dylan followed him, picking up a large bag from the porch.

Chris took a deep breath, hesitated a moment, and sank his key into the lock. Three unsteady breaths later, he crossed the threshold of the musty cabin. Light filtered through the windows, glittering the air, and two sad-looking beds stared at them.

His mom had made those patchwork quilts.

Chris spoke hoarsely, "Still smells of pine and honey and adventure."

Dylan stepped to his side, their arms lightly brushing. "It's been a long time since . . ."

"Why did you ask me here?" Chris whispered.

Dylan threaded their fingers and calmly pulled Chris close.

"I spoke to Mary. She told me how determined you are to keep Bennington Way." His soft voice made Chris's stomach twist. "Why do you hold onto it? You have your parent's house—"

Chris briefly shut his eyes. When he reopened, he glanced at the wall where he used to sit next to Dylan, knees bent, sharing a comic. He looked toward the cold-water shower where they'd shrieked as they washed every morning. The door that they'd stumbled through high, laughing so hard Chris almost pissed himself. The wood where they'd marked their names.

A sharp breath tugged at him, and he stepped backward until he thumped against the door.

"Chris, please. Don't run."

Something tickled his hair. Probably a dust bunny. It moved, and Chris gulped. "Dylan?"

"Yes? You can tell me anything."

"Is there, um, like, something on my head?"

Chris willed himself to move away from the door and shake his hair free of whatever it was, but he couldn't. He'd seized up, and the thought that it could be—

It moved again, touching his neck.

"Get it off, get it off," Chris breathed.

Dylan was already in front of him, his warm presence oozing against Chris's chest, fingers touching his neck. "Just a second, almost got him."

A shudder rippled through him. He slammed his eyes shut. "Please say it's not a spider. Not a spider."

"It's . . . not . . . a spider."

Halsworth still couldn't lie for shit.

"Got it."

The window squealed, and Chris dropped to the floor, shuddering. Dylan returned to the bed, resting his elbows on his thighs and clasping his hands together.

"Thanks," Chris said. "For getting rid of the spider."

"Your harmless garden variety."

He shuffled closer to Dylan. Closer still. At the hiking pack, he stopped. "How long did you plan on waiting for me?"

Dylan opened the clasps on the bag. "As long as it took."

The words stole Chris's breath. He watched Dylan pull out sliced bread and cheese, apples, and—he laughed—a six-pack of Mountain Dew from the bag.

Dylan tossed him a can. They snapped their drinks open at the same time. Chris drank, but Dylan leaned back and rested his on the windowsill.

Gulping down the mouthful of liquid, Chris fiddled with the can ring, then set the drink down.

He slumped next to Dylan on the bed, shoulder-to-shoulder, and the mattress dipped, bringing them closer.

Dylan braced a hand on Chris's leg, close to his knee. A strong, warm pressure. Chris stared at the hand as it drew slowly, lightly up his thigh.

Dylan's shuddering breath whispered over his stubble . . .

Shutting his eyes, Chris leaned toward those lips. Dylan's nose tapped his.

A shiver raced down his arms, down his legs, right to his groin. "I hold onto this place, because it's ours. Every other weekend and holiday, we were here." Chris opened his eyes. Dylan beheld him with tenderness, and it seized Chris's chest. "The kisses matter, Dylan."

Dylan's breath hitched. The softest kiss landed on the corner of Chris's lips. "So, only two-hundred kisses to steal your heart?"

Chris dragged his lips to Dylan's ear. "Only one."

Chapter Twenty-One

DYLAN

DYLAN FELL against the bed at Chris's shove. A hard weight settled on him, and lips peppered his neck with kisses. Salted it with nips of teeth.

"I loved every single one," Chris whispered into the curve between Dylan's neck and shoulders. "Fuck, but you are the most addictive, beautiful, frustrating man I've ever known and I want more of you."

Chris pulled Dylan's hands above his head and laced the fingers of one hand through both of his. He swept a kiss over his lips as he pinned Dylan down.

Tingly warmth settled against his skin and Chris's next kiss sparked like live wires.

Chris held himself rigidly for a breath, and then his weight sagged onto him. "I'm sorry, too, you know," Chris said. "I hurt your feelings back then. I was stupid and scared. I came here that night . . ."

Dylan stilled. "You did?"

"You were sitting on the porch. I wanted to go to you, but . . ." He cleared his throat. "I just couldn't. I knew if I did, I'd screw it up, and then I'd lose my best friend."

"Did you really expect we'd still be friends after you ditched me like that?"

"Yes—no. I knew you'd be mad for a while, but I thought you'd get over it. I was gonna say something, but I wasn't sure how, and then when you caught me kissing McHay—"

"Why did you kiss McHay?"

"I don't know. I was too young for you to be the one. I panicked. I was stupid. You saw us, and got mad, and I yelled at you to wait so I could explain but you didn't, and . . ." Chris loosened his grip on Dylan's hands. "I fucked up. I'm sorry." Chris hauled in a breath and sat up. He stared out the window, his Adam's apple bulging with a swallow.

"What is it?" Dylan asked.

Chris shook his head. There was that vulnerable sixteen-year-old Chris again. Dylan rose onto his elbows, frowning.

"I got so angry you weren't there," Chris said softly, voice cracking. "My parents died, and you were supposed to be there."

Dylan tried to sit up farther, but Chris pressed a light hand to his chest.

"It wasn't you I was really angry at. I was angry at myself for not telling you."

"Chris . . ."

"You cared though. The bench. I didn't know you'd done that."

Dylan wrapped his arms tightly around Chris and pulled him down against his chest. "I'm sorry," he murmured into his hair. "I should have been there. I'm sorry."

THEY STAYED LOCKED IN EACH OTHER'S ARMS FOR CLOSE TO AN hour, watching the last rays of sunset darken to navy. The full moon blared through the windows, and Chris laughed.

"Something funny, Montgomery?" Dylan asked.

Muffled, close to his armpit, Chris said, "Um, so, you know how someone vandalized your floodlight?"

"That was you?" Dylan kissed the top of Chris's head. "Bastard."

"I prefer when you call me sunshine."

"Yeah, you like that?"

Chris pulled back and grinned at him. "Love it. But I'll have you know, if you so much as *think* about replacing that light, I'll do it again. I've got great aim and a killer swing."

Dylan grabbed a fistful of Chris's tank top and yanked him into another kiss, this time arching against the man, letting him feel how much he ached for him.

Chris rubbed their hard groins together, his breath hitching.

Cool fingers crept under his shirt, caressing his skin, playing at the elastic of his briefs. Then slid to the belt. Undid it.

Buttons snapped open, fingers dancing over his hard cock. He groaned, and a smug, beautiful grin lit up Chris's face. He wriggled down his body, grabbing at his jeans as he kissed Dylan's cock through the thin layer of material covering him.

"Stop teasing," Dylan said, threading Chris's hair and angling his head up until they were looking at each other. "It's been long enough, get inside me already. Condom in my wallet. Lube in the backpack."

A blur of action followed. They peeled off their clothes with little ceremony, dumping them in a heap. Chris swore as he searched for supplies and returned with a condom and lube, and a cocky grin. "You prepared, huh?"

"I'm an optimist."

Chris smirked. He knelt between Dylan's legs, his cock standing proudly hard. With another grin, he took himself in hand and stroked, dropping his head back and breathing a low "fuck."

"Cocky, exhibitionist tease," Dylan said, shaking his head. He grabbed his own pulsing cock. "Two can play at that game."

Three firm strokes was all he got in before Chris swiped away his hand. Lowering that cheeky expression, Chris flicked out a tongue at the head of his cock.

Dylan twitched, but his next string of words was stolen from him as Chris suddenly sucked him in deep. Hands explored Dylan's chest and tweaked his nipples as wet heat enveloped him and tightened.

Dylan resisted the urge to thrust his way to a quick release. Damn, he wanted this to last. He wanted to come with Chris—

Chris nuzzled a lubed finger at his entrance and worked his way inside to the rhythm of his sucking mouth.

"Seriously," Dylan groaned. "Inside."

One last agonizingly hot suck, finger fucking him in double time, and Chris drew off him, lips swollen, gaze needy with lust. He reached for the condom nestled at Dylan's ass, ripped open the foil, and rolled it on.

"How much prep you need?" Chris asked, rubbing two fingers at his entrance.

"Forget that, I can handle it." Dylan prepped himself enough on his own.

"Nevertheless. I love watching my fingers"—a blast of sparks flooded him as Chris slid two fingers into him, brushing against his prostate—"disappear into you."

Dylan lifted onto one elbow and hauled Chris into a kiss, wet, hot, hurried. "Do you want me to beg?"

"Well, now that you mention it . . ."

"Sunshine," Dylan warned.

Chris landed a palm on Dylan's chest and pushed him back against the quilt. A predatory aura overtook his eyes as he positioned himself and groaned "fuck, yes" as he stretched Dylan with his cock.

Fisting the sheets, Dylan panted. Chris was inside him. *Chris*.

"God you feel tight around me." Chris dipped for a kiss, and Dylan murmured into it.

"More."

Chris snapped his hips into action, thrusting long and hard, hitting his spot with every stroke.

The bed jerked, banging against the wall.

Chris crushed him with his thrusts, and Dylan loved it. The hard, warm weight pounding into him, the slapping of their bodies, the grunts, the dirty, filthy words bouncing between them, making his skin shiver.

"Fuck, yes."

Their gazes caught, and Chris stared down at him with passion and need and tenderness—

Fully sheathed, Chris leaned forward and kissed him again. "Never get enough of your kisses. Loved them all. Every. Single. One."

A firm squeeze around his cock lit his nerve-endings on fire. Chris stroked in time to his thrusts, working fast, faster—

Chris stiffened. "Dylan."

His name combined with a gently twisted stroke of his cock sent Dylan over the edge. His orgasm shot out of him, rope after rope hitting their chests.

"Oh, God."

Chris sank onto him, their bodies meshing, fitting perfectly together.

Little breaths puffed against his stubble, his cheek, a feeling he hoped he would get used to.

"We're not too young now," Chris said.

"Too young for what?" Dylan grinned. "'Cause I'm not too old. I could go again. In like an hour."

Chris chortled and kissed his shoulder. "I mean, for us to work out. I've never been satisfied with anyone like I am with you. I always hoped to find another Dylan. Another best friend."

Words were trapped behind a large lump in his throat. He drew Chris's face to his and kissed him.

With a grumble, Chris rolled off him and helped Dylan clean up.

When they were come-free and dressed in boxer briefs, Chris snuck in another kiss. And another. Each one soaked into Dylan like sunshine. They traded grins that reminded Dylan of their youth, when they'd share the bed after freaking each other out with ghost stories.

Chris brushed a kiss on Dylan's shoulder. His gaze focused on the windows.

"What are you looking at?"

"I'm too damn stubborn, Dylan. Thank you for asking me here."

"I wasn't sure you'd come." Dylan laughed and bumped their noses lightly together.

Chris drew Dylan nearer and nipped his lips. "One thing before we start round two."

"What's that?"

Chris blushed. "Can I help out at camp some more? You know, maybe run a baseball session or ten?"

A deep smile pulled at Dylan. "You really do love having kids around. Mr. Montgomery, you're full of surprises."

"That's a yes?"

"More than a yes, Chris. It's a promise."

Chapter Twenty-Two

CHRISTMAS

CHRIS

Christmas day had Chris dragging Dylan out into the snowplowed yard toward his boat shed. The shed he'd kept the man out of for months. No easy feat.

"It's done? I can finally see?" Dylan grinned.

Chris swallowed a smirk and tugged Dylan into the shed. A tarpaulin cloaked his mahogany runabout.

"I never thought I'd see the day you'd let me in here." Dylan curiously rounded the covered boat. "Can I take a peek?"

Chris uncovered the beauty.

Dylan blinked several times in awe. His Adam's apple jutted, and his eyes beheld Chris softly. "You named your boat after me?"

"Seemed right. It, too, is a one and only."

Dylan laughed and reached out to touch the bow. "Can I?"

"Yeah. But I need you to promise something, Halsworth."

"What's that, Montgomery?"

A shared grin. "I want to take you out in it sometime—"

"Will you let me drive?"

Chris snorted. "No."

"What?" Dylan pouted.

"Dude, I love you, right, but you suck at driving boats."

Dylan faced him sharply. "What did you say?"

"I said you suck at driving."

Dylan backed him up against the runabout. Their noses met. The kiss curled Chris's toes. "I love you, too."

ALSO AVAILABLE

HOW TO EVICT A HOT JOCK IN THREE WEEKS
How to Love #2

THE UPTIGHT CURATOR . . .

Let's list all the reasons why Logan Stone is the worst roommate for Alexander Kress to share his beloved house with.

He:

🐀 loves possum (over-sized rodent) for dinner

🐛 keeps worms in the fridge and hunts fishes with a spear

🚚 thinks monster trucks are theatre

😉 is clearly hiding something behind that twinkle in his eye

Plus he's straight—and sexy. And Alexander needs to stop *shivering*.

THE CHEEKY THESPIAN . . .

Logan couldn't have scripted it better.

Just one more day of obnoxious shenanigans and Alexander would evict his method-acting ass. Except, maybe he needs two days. Maybe a few more—

What is this man made of?

It's almost like . . .

Shit. The cute curator knows what he's up to. But he doesn't *know* Logan knows he knows . . .

Wait. Back up. Did he just say *cute*?

How To Evict A Hot Jock in Three Weeks is a standalone opposites attract, hero-in-disguise, bisexual realization rom-com.

Anyta Sunday

HEART-STOPPING SLOW BURN

A bit about me: I'm a big, BIG fan of slow-burn romances. I love to read and write stories with characters who slowly fall in love.

Some of my favorite tropes to read and write are: Enemies to Lovers, Friends to Lovers, Clueless Guys, Bisexual, Pansexual, Demisexual, Oblivious MCs, Everyone (Else) Can See It, Slow Burn, Love Has No Boundaries.

I write a variety of stories, Contemporary MM Romances with a good dollop of angst, Contemporary lighthearted MM Romances, and even a splash of fantasy.
My books have been translated into German, Italian, French, Spanish, and Thai.

Contact: http://www.anytasunday.com/about-anyta/
Sign up for Anyta's newsletter and receive a free e-book:
http://www.anytasunday.com/newsletter-free-e-book/

Join my Facebook group to chat all things Slow Burn Romance:
https://www.facebook.com/groups/SlowBurnSundays/

You can also find me here:
www.anytasunday.com
anytasunday@gmail.com

For information about new releases and freebies, follow me on BookBub:
https://www.bookbub.com/authors/anyta-sunday

www.ingramcontent.com/pod-product-compliance
Lightning Source LLC
LaVergne TN
LVHW041502190726
843491LV00008B/2498
* 9 7 8 3 9 4 7 9 0 9 2 5 4 *